EYEGLASS JOURNEYS

A whimsical tale of truth, fiction, and fantasy

EYEGLASS JOURNEYS

SUSAN WARD DELAURENTIS

MANY**SEASONS**PRESS

Mesa, Arizona • 2020

FIRST EDITION

EYEGLASS JOURNEYS
A whimsical tale of truth, fiction, and fantasy

Copyright © 2020 by Susan Ward DeLaurentis

Published by Many Seasons Press
(An Imprint of MultimediaPublishingProject.com)
PO Box 50553
Mesa, AZ 85208
480.939.9689 | ManySeasonsPress.com

Cover & book interior designed by Yolie Hernandez
(AZBookDesigner@icloud.com)

Paperback ISBN 13: 978-1-936885-34-3
Hardcover ISBN 13: 978-1-936885-38-1

Printed in the United States of America.

To my loving, wonderful, crazy fun family!
Please remember that family is everything.

Dear Jordan,
    I hope when you read this, I am celeb... big day with... I'm looking do... above, know... is with you...
    I had... pillow made... of my wedding... can be your "...
    As I... are 9 years o... remember h... hours old.

PREFACE

never thought I could love someone more than Paul, the man I married 47 years ago. Then, we had children. The overwhelming love you feel for your children is hard to believe. Your heart just seems to grow larger! But then, you have grandchildren.

Paul and I were whisked away by immense surprise. We never imagined the joy a tiny human being, a grandchild, could bring. Our hearts were filled to bursting when we held our first "grand."

I was very close to my maternal grandmother, and I miss her still. I know she loved me. Just as I remember my grandmother, I also want my grandchildren to remember my great love for them. So, I wondered, how could I make this happen?

One of the first things I did with that purpose in mind, was to give my wedding dress to my good friend Cindy, an accomplished seamstress. I asked her to make four pillows from the train and lace of my dress. I boxed each pillow with a picture of me wearing the dress on my wedding day. I also included a note personalized to each one of my grandchildren. This is just in case I'm not with them on their special day.

Then came the day that Paul and I downsized our home and possessions. The one thing I could not part with was my collection of antique eyeglasses. I've been collecting eyeglasses and related paraphernalia for years. I was after all an ophthalmic assistant for 22 years, and wore eyeglasses since the age of six.

I always had my collection displayed throughout my home. I began thinking, what would become of this collection when I'm gone? I realized that if I didn't do something with my eyeglasses now, my children and grandchildren may not be interested in preserving it. They will probably sell them for pennies at an estate sale.

For a few weeks, my mind turned this conundrum over and over. Then, one day, during the wee hours of the morning, when sleep is so elusive, I thought about something creative to do with my eyeglass collection. Why not write a story that incorporates my travels with my eyeglasses?

Paul and I were lucky enough to own motorhomes for over 20 years. We traveled to all 48 contiguous states. We also traveled outside the country to Europe, the Caribbean, Alaska, Hawaii, and more. During those years I was sure we would forget altogether, or begin to jumble, our many memories about these trips, so I began keeping a journal from the very first trip, and continued journaling up until our last excursion in October 2019.

I hope my readers enjoy my whimsical tale. It is a tapestry of truth, fiction, and fantasy. While this book was written for our children, Paul Jr. and Philip, and the gems they fathered, I hope other parents and grandparents find this story inspiring. I'm hoping this leads you to pass on your legacy of love. This was my way of doing that.

To my grandchildren Faith, Jordan, Braylon, and Logan, may you live, love, and laugh often. Remember, Nonna loves you more.

CANADA
Edmonton
Vancouver
Winnipeg
Quebec
Seattle
Portland
Minneapolis
Detroit
Toronto
Chicago
New York
Denver
Washington
San Francisco
UNITED STATES
Los Angeles
Dallas
MEXICO
Havana
CUBA
THE
Mexico City
Port-au-Prince
Kingston
BELIZE
Belmopan
GUATEMALA
HONDURAS
Guatemala
Tegucigalpa
NICARAGUA
Managua
San Jose
PANAMA
COSTA RICA
Panama
Bogota
COLOMBIA

PART ONE

EYEGLASS JOURNEYS

We **called our grandmother Nonna.** She passed away suddenly when I was 14. A few months after she was laid to rest, our Pop-Pop asked my dad, sister, Uncle Philip, and my cousins to his home for dinner. We talked a lot about Nonna and after dessert, Pop pulled out four large packages. One package for each of her grandchildren—me, Faith, my sis Jordan, age 12, and my twin cousins, Braylon and Logan, ages 11.

Pop-Pop explained that Nonna had divided her collection of antique eyeglasses between us, the four grandchildren. We all knew that Nonna collected unique pairs of eyeglasses over many years. She displayed them with cases, and different types of eyeglass paraphernalia all over her home. As kids, none of us were very impressed with this collection, but they were a part of her, so we were happy to have them.

None of us could have expected the inexplicable journeys that were to come!

FAITH

bring the glasses Pop-Pop gave me to my bedroom. I am about to park them in the back of my closet, but then I decide to take a look at my new collection. I was very happy to see that Nonna had remembered that as a little girl, I played with a very avant-garde lorgnette. This is a pair of eyeglasses with a handle. *Avant-Garde* is a French term meaning vanguard, so these glasses were a kind of new and fashionable trend back in the day. They have a "cat's eye" look with little crystals in the frame. She kept them on a gold-colored stand, which added to the romantic look.

Reflexively, I hold the glasses to my eyes. Immediately, and surprisingly, I see huge mountains against a clear blue sky! I am standing in a green field and, what? Is that a buffalo ambling toward me? I rip the glasses off my face and sit on my bed in disbelief. After a minute, I run to the bathroom, splash water on my face and wipe my eyes. Back in my bedroom, I close the door, return to my bed and reset the glasses. Was that vision of a beautiful landscape and a buffalo real or am I having an early-age onset stroke?

After the initial shock, I decided to look through the glasses once again hoping it was all in my head, but nope, I am still seeing a bison! I also begin hearing birds and insects. I can feel the sun on my skin and breathe the cool, clean air. Taking down the lorgnette, I see that I am still in my bedroom. I take stock of, well, me. I feel fine. So what is happening? Why and how am I seeing all of this?

I leave my room looking for answers to these questions. As casually as I can, I find my dad and ask if I could look at Nonna's journals. Dad was in the process of reading them. He told Pop-Pop that he would scan them to flash drives so everyone in the family would have a copy. Nonna and Pop-Pop traveled extensively over their 47 years together. Whether she was traveling the United States in their RV or touring cities in Europe, Nonna wrote about all of it in her journals. This was a great idea since the journals helped them remember details about the places they visited. My grandparents had also spent months working in Yellowstone National Park. This huge wild recreational area, located mostly in Wyoming and parts of Montana and Idaho, is famous for its alpine rivers, canyons, hot springs, gushing geysers, lush forests, not to mention its animals. They spoke often of the large herds of bison that roamed the park.

As I read Nonna's journal, I want to find an entry regarding their arrival at Yellowstone, something that would seem familiar about the scene I was experiencing through the glasses. I finally find a journal entry dated 4/29/17. *"We are entering Yellowstone National Park through the West gate. We are immediately greeted by*

Yellowstone

a small herd of bison ambling beside the river and the road." Wow! Nonna's description is exactly what I am seeing when I put on the "magic" glasses!

As my curiosity and awe grows, I spend the next several days alternately looking through those lenses and reading my Nonna's "views" of Yellowstone. Amazingly, I watch as my eyes take me through the most beautiful landscapes I have ever seen. I stand before the magnificent Lower Falls, which I learn is the tallest waterfall in Yellowstone. I watch the waters crash down 308 feet, and feel the power emanate from the rocks below. Excitedly, I sit on the benches surrounding Old Faithful, a geyser. I watch along with the crowds and see the most famous geyser in the world. It does not disappoint. Boiling water is emitted with great force about 150 feet into the air! I listen as a park ranger explains that the geyser erupts approximately every 90 minutes.

Later, I find myself climbing the switchbacks to the top of Bunsen Peak, at 8,500 feet, and I see views that seem to go on forever. A new-growth forest carpets the hillsides surrounding Swan Lake Flat as graceful antelope drink at the water's edge.

I can't believe my eyes, or I should say my glasses, as I take in the intense colors of the Grand Prismatic Spring, the largest hot spring in Yellowstone. Oranges, yellows, blues, and greens, all held within a labyrinth of wooden boardwalks. I can feel the heat while watching the steam rise.

Over the next few days, I became familiar with so much of the wildlife that exists within Yellowstone's amazing ecosystem. I watched while a mama grizzly bear taught her twin cubs to forage. The bison mommies were very protective of the calves that had been born in the spring. Bison calves are called "red dogs" due to the beautiful red dirt coloring they have until their first birthday! Too cute!! I also saw the adult male elks lock horns while their harem of females looked on. And all of this was documented by my Nonna. She always told me that her Yellowstone experience was something she would never forget. Now, she is passing it on to me. She left me so much more than antique eyeglasses. She gave me her true love of adventure and a strong desire to explore the world. I am also sure these "magical" eyeglass journeys are happening because she loved me best!

JORDAN

'm so sure I'm the only one of us that is excited to receive Nonna's gift! The entire drive home, I am anxious to open the package. Ever since I was a child, I had been drawn to a shadowbox that hung in Nonna's house on a wall. She had created a beautiful display for her most prized piece, a sterling silver chatelaine. One time she explained that the chatelaine is similar to a modern-day tool belt. Chatelaines were worn by women for hundreds of years past. These belts were used to carry household items like scissors or, of course, eyeglasses.

I race to my room and open the package. There it is. The shadowbox is wooden, and it is backed with black velvet. The ornately decorated chatelaine's interior is lined with silk, and peeking out is the most delicate pair of glasses I have ever seen. I remove the back of the box's frame and release the glasses from their intricate case. The specs are so dainty, and I take special care to unfold them. Nonna had explained that she had purchased these glasses online from an eBay seller in France. The seller described the chatelaine as once being part of a family estate sale, and as a piece from the 1700s. Nonna paid a "pretty penny" for the cherished item. I know she meant for me to have it, because for sure she loved me best!!

I remove the glass from the front of the shadowbox, replace the black velvet backing and hang the display on the wall behind my bed. I run my fingers along the beautiful molds of the silver. It makes me feel close to Nonna.

Then came the day I decide I want to see what I look like in these thin-framed glasses. So after carefully pulling the glasses' arms around my ears, I open my eyes and see what I know to be the Eiffel Tower! Holy heck! These aren't normal glasses. They seem like virtual reality goggles! But wait...wow, I am walking on a sidewalk that is cutting through a park-like setting. I look up to see the sun shining over the top of this world-famous wrought iron structure, built in the late 1800s. I remember Nonna and Pop-Pop talking about their visit to Paris, France in Europe. Nonna claimed that seeing the Eiffel Tower was a highlight of all her travels. Paris is the capital and the most populated city in France, and lies to the north.

I continue walking towards the tower and then I enter the elevator. It looks like I'm going to the top! Wow! The views are clear, and I can see for miles and miles. I look down on perfectly blocked gardens and parks. I also see roads crossing and crisscrossing through the town in all directions. I begin to experience sensory overload, so I gingerly take off the glasses. I am back in my room. What is happening? Did I just experience Paris?

France

My dad has all of Nonna's travel journals on his desk downstairs. I run downstairs and begin looking through them, it takes quite a while, but I find the notes Nonna wrote about her Paris trip dated 3/15/02. All the journals were written in cursive handwriting. Beautiful, but very difficult to read. Her entries about the Eiffel Tower are spot on as to what I witnessed through these glasses. I just experienced Paris through her eyes!

Over the next few days, I follow the journal entries, and with the glasses on, I view the exact places that Nonna observed. I come face to face with the Italian artist Leonardo da Vinci's Mona Lisa oil painting. Housed in The Louvre, this masterpiece, painted in 1503, is just one of the many paintings, statues, artifacts, and sculptures found in the world's largest art museum. I am thrilled to be standing in the same halls walked by Marie Antoinette in the Versailles Palace. I also find myself taking a guided tour of the Hall of Mirrors and the Royal Opera House. At one point, I am drinking a diet soda at a McDonald's restaurant in Paris! Who knew?

Another notable visit was to a century-old cafe, *Angelina*, known for their famous hot chocolate. Just as Nonna had written, the hot chocolate is served in a pitcher. In front of me is an ice cream sundae glass, filled with real whipped cream. It was needed to "cut" the thickness of the chocolate! This eyeglass journey doesn't cease to amaze me!

Strolling along the Champs-Elysées, I am filled with awe as "the world's most beautiful avenue" is teaming with people speaking every different language. A metropolitan melting pot to be sure. I reach the Arc de Triomphe, the most imposing of the city's arches. I take the underground tunnel to get across the undulating circle of traffic, just as my grandmother had noted in her journal.

I am navigating a very small street, and now I am standing next to a tiny crepe stand. I am eating the most delicious crepe that was just made for me. The thin pancake-like dough is filled with strawberries, whipped cream, and Nutella spread. I wonder, are there virtual reality calories?

I seem to be getting off the Paris rapid transit system now, the Métro, where I can see the famous Moulin Rouge, with its iconic windmill. I would recognize it anywhere because I watched the movie, Moulin Rouge with Nonna several times. According to the map I picked up on the train, I am now in the district of Montmartre.

My grandmother noted two grand churches on her journey. So I know as I am climbing to the highest point in Montmartre, that I am seeing the Sacré-Coeur Basilica. From the base of the steps, I look up and see the three-domed cathedral with its bronze statues of Joan of Arc and King Louis IV on horseback.

Notre Dame is the other famous cathedral she notes. Because of the name, I thought this was a school in the United States. Again, who knew? I can see why she took note of this grand building. The rose windows that she thought colorful are my favorite as I wander down the enormous center aisle. The altar, the ceilings, and stained glass are amazing. Everything is opulent, to say the least!

It has been a whirlwind! Even though I haven't left my bedroom, I'm exhausted. I have no clue as to how any of these amazing, virtual adventures are possible, but I do know that I need to learn French!   *Je t'aime* Nonna!

BRAYLON

I'm in the fifth grade and I have been given a school project concerning the American Civil War. We've studied some of the basics in class, but I have some research to do. My dad was asking me about the project, when he remembered his mom had a pair of glasses, and a case that she had been told was from the "Civil War era."

To tell the truth, I am not interested in Nonna's eyeglass collection. Dad knows my brother and I are too young to care, so he stashed the packages Pop-Pop gave us months ago. But now, I can see and feel that there may be a connection. Dad and I look through each individually wrapped piece. Number six is the charm! A hammered tin case encloses a thin silver-colored frame with oval lenses. Over 150 years ago, a soldier in the Civil War could have held this exact item! Amazing that it stood the test of time.

Dad helps me photograph Nonna's find for the project. As he is about to package the specs and case back up, I ask him if I can keep them in my room until my paper is complete. I want to "see" that connection to the past every day. Over the next week or so I write and rewrite my paper. I decided to focus on the ten most critical battles of this four-year war, from 1861 to 1865. It was a lot of work, but I enjoyed learning about such a complicated time in our nation's history.

Weeks pass and the paper with its big red "A" sits below the Civil War era glasses that have become my new paperweight. It's Saturday and dad is on my butt to clean my room. Naturally, I am doing anything to delay the chore. I pick up the eyeglasses and curl the thin wire frames around my ears. Pushing the bridge up on my nose, I see that I am looking down, very far down! I'm on a horse. No, really. I am on a horse that is trudging on the brink of a dirt trail. I look out and see what can only be described as a landscape filled with enormous melting orange Creamsicle bars. They are melting because it must be 100 degrees, and the sun is baking me alive!

Carefully taking off the glasses, I find that I am in my room—no horse. It's the glasses! I quickly put them back on, and no doubt about it. I am part of a long trail of people on horseback. One false move by my horse and I'm a goner! My fear is overcome by wonder, however, as I look at views of what I later learned are hoodoos. These red, orange, and white-colored geological structures are so distinctive. A guide is giving a tour, and I learn that we are descending about 8,500 feet to the base of Bryce Canyon National Park, in southwestern Utah. My horse is much calmer than I am, so I relax in the saddle and ride it out.

Bryce Canyon

Our guide tells tales of Native American habitation in this region for at least 10,000 years. The rock formations are so unusual and colorful that they are not duplicated anywhere else on the entire planet! The geology has formed rock into bridges, arches, and towering walls. Just like people find the familiar in clouds, I see shapes in the hoodoos that remind me of castles, people, and animals. We see formations that have names like Thor's Hammer, The Poodle, Chinese Wall, Queen Victoria, and Sinking Ship.

I am stunned and just cannot go any farther. Putting the glasses away, I find I have been "experiencing" this journey for over an hour. The only people I know that have been to Bryce Canyon are Nonna and Pop-Pop. My Uncle Paul had all of Nonna's journals and pictures put on a flash drive for my dad. I need to find that flash drive.

It's midnight now and dad is asleep. I know that he keeps a lockbox in the hall closet. I find it and start punching in numbers for the lock code. His birthday, of course! I need to talk to Dad about his lack of security. Got it! The lockbox opens.

The computer is in the living room, and I pop the drive into the slot. Nonna's cursive handwriting appears. Yikes! I don't have all night. So I go to the picture files instead. Within 15 minutes I find pictures of everything I've seen through the eyeglasses, including Nonna and Pop-Pop atop very large horses!

Now I'm hooked! I have to find Bryce in the journals. An hour in and I see it. Nonna wrote, Tuesday, 5/23/00... "Bryce is total eye candy." Nonna goes on to describe their hike from rim to base on the Queen's Garden and Navajo Loop trails. *"We hike through incredible 'Wall Street' where the red/orange colored walls rise so high you feel as if you are in a cathedral."* She writes about the views and 13 different viewpoints on a drive around the rim of the canyon. Between the drive, hike, and the horseback tour, my grandparents saw it all.

How am I seeing all of this through a flimsy pair of glasses? Now, I'm a self-professed gamer, so virtual reality isn't a new concept to me. But this? A 150-year-old pair of eyeglasses?

Looking at the clock, I see that I have been glued to the computer screen for three hours. I rush to put everything away and jump into bed.

Sunday mornings' light peaks through the window blinds. It's 10:00 a.m. and I am surprised to feel wide awake. I cannot wait to get a few hours to myself so I can connect again with Nonna's past adventure. I now know what I always suspected: I was Nonna's favorite grandkid!!

LOGAN

Dad and Braylon are looking at the eyeglasses Nonna left us both. They are working on Bray's school project. I am gaming at this time, but before dad packs up the specs, I take my half into my bedroom and start looking at the eyeglasses. One pair of "Harry Potter" glasses call to me. I'm not a Potter fan but I remember seeing these glasses at Nonna and Pop's house. Except for this pair, the glasses are much older-looking with thin frames that I feel I might break if I'm not careful.

I go to the mirror and put on the Potter's. I want to satisfy my curiosity as to what I would look like in glasses. Up to now, I have perfect vision. My dad had laser eye surgery and my mom wears contact lenses, so I'm thinking at some point I may need to wear these things.

I naturally expect to see my bedroom when I look up, but instead, I am looking down from a bicycle seat. Holy crap! There is an alligator right next to me! Ahhhhh!!! I rip off the glasses

Everglades

and jump onto my bed. OMG! I take a good look at the glasses and they are perfectly normal, boring, black-framed glasses. I place the specs carefully on my nose and again I know I am on a bike staring down at a full-fledged alligator! It has rough skin and is very long. His eyes are closed, and he seems to be asleep. My heart is pounding as I "push the pedal to the metal," and tear off down the path. Where am I and why am I seeing and feeling all of this?

Again, off come the glasses. I'm in my bedroom and I grab my iPad. "Where do alligators live in the US?" I type. The answer pops up immediately—the southeastern United States. I read, "The largest alligator population lives in Louisiana, but they are also found in Oklahoma, Texas, Arkansas, Mississippi, Alabama, North and South Carolina, Georgia and Florida." Now I think to Google the words, "bike path plus alligator." Shark Valley Trail, Everglades National Park, Florida appears on the screen. There is even a picture of two bikes propped up right next to an alligator, looking identical to what I am seeing through the Potter glasses. I learn that Everglades National Park lies in the very southern region of Florida's tip.

Okay, the glasses belonged to Nonna, and I know that she and Pop-Pop spent lots of travel time in Florida. I have to find out if they were on this bike trail. Uncle Paul had all of Nonna's journals scanned and put on a flash drive. My dad has this drive in a lockbox. I genuinely don't want to tell dad what I am seeing. I'm afraid that if I say anything, the "magic" will cease!

After some thought, I realize that I'm seeing all of this because of Nonna. I was always sure she loved me best, but now I am certain!

The next day, Braylon has boxing practice after school, and I'm home alone while dad is at work. I know where the lockbox is kept. I spied on dad once and saw that the combination was his birthday. Lame. I grab the drive and pop it in the computer.

Holy crap! I read so many entries. Reading takes forever as I try to decipher Nonna's cursive handwriting. I look for the word 'Florida,' and power through each page. The downside is that they visited Florida a lot. I decide to look for the word 'alligator,' and finally find the exact description of being on the bike. My grandmother was describing the alligator adventure on the Shark Valley Trail. Yes! Racing back to my room I again put on the "Potter" glasses.

It is a beautiful sunny day with clear skies and wow, am I hot! It is even more humid than my old neighborhood in North Carolina. I feel more comfortable on the bike now since I know that Nonna and Pop-Pop survived this trail. I'm following Nonna's writings in my mind, and I know I'm on a 15-mile biking trail which will lead to a 65-foot-high observation tower. Around me I see miles of sawgrass and in one area the path travels alongside a water-filled canal. All along the path, I see alligators but also egrets, storks, ibis, and heron. The alligators mix throughout the trail with the birds. I am guessing these alligators are not interested in feeding. They seem lethargic at best.

I finally come to the concrete observation tower, park the bike and climb to the top. Holy crap! I get a spectacular view. Below me on all sides are dozens of alligators. They are side to side, nose to tail, and nestled in the green, moist sawgrass below.

I am hot and tired but exhilarated at the same time. Taking off the specs, I realize that I want to see more. I start to look through Nonna's journal and begin reading about places they traveled to and the great things they saw. I'm thinking that I want to travel too when I am finished with all the school I have ahead of me. Now I start to think of something else. Will this transport happen again if I put on a different pair of glasses? Nonna and Pop-Pop traveled so much over their 47 years together. I cannot wait to see what comes next.

CANADA
Edmonton
Vancouver
Seattle
Portland
Winnipeg
Québec
Minneapolis
Detroit
Toronto
Chicago
New York
Denver
Washington
San Francisco
UNITED STATES
Dallas
MEXICO
Havana
CUBA
Mexico City
THE BAHAMAS
Port-au-Prince
BELIZE
Belmopan
GUATEMALA
HONDURAS
Guatemala
Tegucigalpa
NICARAGUA
Managua
San José
PANAMA
COSTA RICA
Panama
Bogotá
COLOMBIA

PART TWO

FAITH

t has been a magical six months. I have seen so many "off the beaten track" areas of Yellowstone National Park through Nonna's lorgnette.

It sounds crazy now, but it was quite a while until I thought about the other glasses Pop-Pop gave me! The day I did consider them, I was awed to find that four other pairs of glasses allowed me to virtually travel. I have also been able to find all the places I visit in Nonna's journals.

I found what looked like a monocle —a single eyeglass— a silver Pince-nez attached to a long chain that I hang around my neck. Pince-nez glasses are armless and fit tightly on the nose; they were much in style about one hundred years ago.

These specs get me to Estes Park, Colorado, another western state. I am in a car and the scenery is beautiful with tall aspens and their golden shimmering leaves on all sides. Slowly, I travel up a twisting road in the Rocky Mountains. Nonna's journal dated this trip on 9/23/01. As I travel up to 12,000 feet, the wind is blowing hard and the temps are dropping. There is no guard rail and my stomach knots as I look over the road's edge. One false move... At this height and climate, I am witnessing tundra, an area where no trees grow. It is stark and I am thankful to be going back down the mountain!

Nonna also gave me a gold Pince-nez that has an attached gold-colored chain with a large hairpin. These glasses take me to Key West, Florida. Key West is the southernmost city in the contiguous US. According to Nonna's writings, she and Pop-Pop spent lots of time there over the years. I experience the trip they took in February 2006. I'm riding through the narrow streets on a scooter. It looks like this mode of transportation is the best way to maneuver the crowded streets. The best part of this trip happens at dusk. I view an amazing sunset over the turquoise, clear water. I have never seen oranges so orange! Yellows, soft blues, and tints of pink. Almost mystical.

I see more adventures while wearing a frameless octagonal pair of glasses with a distinctive yellow tint and I find myself surrounded by blue skies and fine white sand. I am lounging on a chair at the water's edge. The water is clear and crystalline blue! You can see the sandy bottom of the surf. To my left, I notice a gentleman walking toward me with an ear to ear smile. He is dressed in what looks like a waiter's uniform. He asks if he can get me a refreshment and I ask for a soda. Where am I? When the soft drink is delivered, the napkin with it reads, "San Souci." I find out later that this is a popular resort on the island of Jamaica. Wow. This location is heavenly! I spend the next few hours snorkeling the refreshing waters, swimming with

CONCH
REPUBLIC
90 Miles to Cuba
THE
SOUTHERNMOST
POINT
CONTINENTAL
U.S.A.
KEY WEST FL

every color fish I can imagine. I walk the grounds and take in the enormous green foliage and breathtaking flowers. The floral fragrance floats lightly on the breeze. I need to come back here often! Looking at an atlas, I find Jamaica in the Caribbean Sea. This island country lies to the east of the United States.

My last "journey" is courtesy of a tiny pair of dark sunglasses with thin wire frames. I find myself in a place that looks nothing like I have ever seen before. The buildings, the streets; everything looks so old. I also notice that everyone around me is speaking with a British accent. I'm in London, England! Wow! The journal confirms it. My grandparents, along with friends, went to England in March 2002. This country is in North-West Europe.

According to the people all around me, I am about to see the changing of the guard. I am standing at the front of Buckingham Palace, where Queen Elizabeth II lives. What pomp and circumstance. Later, I am on a tour boat gliding down the Thames, a river that flows through southern England, listening to information about its history. The marks of civilization date back to pre-Roman times. The river was used for all manner of shipping. Today, the river is used extensively for recreation as well.

Browsing through the journals, I see that Nonna has recorded notes about family memories as well, and I find one about me! *"Faith is growing so fast and standing. She has four teeth and is chewing everything."* Wow, I was not even one-year-old at that time.

Today, though, I am lying on my bed thinking about the truly unbelievable travel experiences these glasses have given me. I'm wondering if Jordan's glasses allow her this same freaky experience. I'm thinking I should tell my dad about the glasses, but what if he can't see what I see? I decide that I have to find out about Jordan's glasses first. Later that night, I learn all I need to know.

Dad is watching TV and I'm coloring in a sketch I am working on when Jordan walks through the door from karate practice. She says hi, and then tells us she needs to get homework done and goes up to her bedroom. Minutes later, I notice that her backpack with her schoolbooks is still by the front door. How is she doing homework without her books?

I climb the stairs quietly. I open her bedroom door and see her sitting on her bed, staring as if in a trance through a very old-looking pair of glasses. Well, I didn't need a complicated plan, I just needed to open her door! I now know that she too can "see" Nonna's journal entries come to life!

JORDAN

My Paris escapade was amazing. Every time I put those glasses on, I relive that wild journey. Being the inquisitive type however, it wasn't long before I began trying on all the other eyeglasses I had been given. Four more specs gave me views into diverse and interesting locales that had been toured by my grandparents.

A tiny pair of bright blue colored sunglasses affords me a "trip" to Savannah, Georgia, where I find myself on a trolley tour of this old-world town. Georgia is an east coast state in the United States. Large, gracious homes line the streets, but the magnificent trees are what I am awed by most. Grand mighty oaks rise to great heights with Spanish moss hanging dramatically from almost every limb. I am sure it hasn't changed much since Nonna was there in March 2000.

A pair of round black framed glasses, allow me to spend an entire day experiencing Grand Canyon National Park in

northwestern Arizona. My grandparents took this trip in the fall of 2010.

I am standing in a tiny airport holding a ticket for the "Grand Canyon West" tour. Our tour group boards a small airplane which takes us high above Hoover Dam and Lake Mead recreational area. Seeing the waters and the mountains from above is a sight I won't forget. Stunning! No wonder the Grand Canyon is one of the seven natural wonders of the world!

The next part of the trip is by helicopter. We are all given headphones so we can hear the guide over the sound of the whirlybird. Wow is this thing LOUD.

We land next to the Colorado River, which carved out the Grand Canyon eons ago. We step onto a pontoon boat which glides through the calm waters. We are surrounded on both sides by towering cliffs.

Now we are boarding a tour bus taking us through the canyon to Eagle Point on the western rim. Our guide explains that we are on the Hualapai reservation. This land is owned by this Native American tribe and not part of the national park. We are permitted to stroll through a traditionally built village.

Nonna's pictures could never do this incredible trip justice. After seeing the canyon from the air, the river and at ground level, I am truly grateful to my grandparents. They are opening my eyes to the wonders of nature.

Dated "May 2000" I found Nonna's description of their stay in Sedona, Arizona, in the southwestern portion of the U.S. I see the red sandstone rock through an unusual Pince-nez that folds in on itself. Press the lenses together and it springs open to become a lorgnette with a silver filigree handle! I travel up a winding hill to Chapel of the Holy Cross. This chapel is built right into the hillside and takes advantage of the views. Sedona's red rock mountains, whimsical formations, and a picture-perfect sky take my breath away.

My last experience is seen through a pair of gold glasses that have some unusual details. First, the nosepiece and arms have gold that is twisted like a rope. At the very top outer corner of each lens there are tiny decorations of crystals. Very mid-twentieth century! Through these specs I can stand on a cliff at Acadia National Park in Maine. I look out over the Atlantic Ocean. I get to experience Thunder Hole, where the sea crashes against the rocky shores. It does thunder, just as Nonna recorded from their trip dated "August 2000." Another noteworthy item in Acadia National Park is a hike up a very difficult trail. This entire mountain is granite and I reach the top only by climbing a series of metal ladders and rungs permanently placed. Mounting the summit I find views that let you know the difficulty was worth the climb. Dark green forested mountains surround you. As I begin my descent, I get a tap on my shoulder which propels me right off my bed. I rip the glasses off my face. OMG, it's Faith! I can tell by her smirk that she knows exactly what I'm up to...

FAITH

Jordan bounces off her bed, her eyes wide and a look on her face that expresses, "caught." We talk and discover that we are both able to "travel" courtesy of Nonna's amazing collection of glasses. We compare notes on our different experiences. We have so many questions, and pepper each other with one after another.

We look through the original journals that Dad shared with us, and highlight the places we have seen through Nonna's eyeglasses. We are surprised to find that we each see different locations. Next, I take the glasses from the chatelain hanging on Jordan's wall. Expecting to see Paris, I am shocked to find that all I can see is Jordan's bedroom! I grab the lorgnette through which I experience Yellowstone and hand them to my sister. As Jordan peers through the lenses she breaks into a huge smile. She sees bison! Why is she able to see through my glasses, but I can't see Paris through her glasses? I hand her the tiny sunglasses and she should see the beautiful blue Jamaican waters. But, she only sees a beautiful blue bedroom wall!

For the next hour we try on every pair of glasses we own between us. Nothing. The only pair of glasses we both "experience" through is the tortoiseshell lorgnette. We can both visit Yellowstone National Park and that's all. We are stumped.

Now, however, a new question comes to mind. I ask Jordan if she thinks we should speak to our cousins about their specs? Wow. How do we even begin this conversation? Have they even looked at the glasses they received or are the glasses collecting dust somewhere in their house? If we talk to them about this, will it break some sort of spell, and the eyeglass journeys' "miracle" come to an end? If only Jordan and I can be transported, will the boys be upset with Nonna?

We decide that we have to know. This weekend we will all be together at Uncle Philip's home to watch the Eagles football game. Since Jordan always carries a purse, we will smuggle in the Yellowstone, Paris and Jamaica glasses for testing. We just have to know.

BRAYLON

I love watching the Eagles games. Win or lose, the DeLaurentis family bleeds green. So I wasn't too happy that Sunday, when Faith insisted that we talk "in private." I reluctantly invite her and Jordan into my room. Faith closes the door with a determined look in her eyes. Then she drops the bomb by asking if I have ever looked at the package of glasses Pop-Pop gave to us from Nonna.

I knew right away that I would finally be able to share my fantastical story of virtual reality touring! I felt somewhat relieved. I unloaded the secret that I had kept from everyone. I didn't stop talking until I related every detail of the trips taken courtesy of Nonna. Beside my Bryce Canyon trail ride with the Civil War era glasses, I have "visited" four other places. Each time I am transported by a different pair of glasses.

A gold Pince-nez eyepiece has a short gold chain attached to a widely shaped gold wire that wraps around the ear. While

wearing it I am transported to Ricketts Glen, a state park in Pennsylvania. I start at the highest point of the Falls Loop trail and descend past 21 waterfalls. I am guessing it is Springtime as each of the waterfalls are thunderous. I find a large stick which I use to navigate the rocky trail. The land surrounding this trail is dense with trees. The sun barely peeks through the thick foliage. Each waterfall is so different. Some falls are tall while others are shorter in height but longer, as the water flows over boulders and rocks. I stop every once in a while to dip my toes into the cold, clear water. Although the trail is quite long, I am invigorated and hungry! I have built up one big appetite. I pick out a big flat rock and in my backpack, I find a peanut butter and jelly sandwich. I look on my phone and find that Ricketts Glen is only a few hours north of our home! I think I see a road trip in my family's future!

I find a metal pair of glasses that has a strange folding mechanism. The arms are hinged and slide to fold. While wearing them, I focus in on the largest archaeological ruin I have ever seen! It is a warm and sunny day. I am part of a swarm of people speaking foreign languages. Thankfully, I find myself to be part of a tour and the guide is speaking English. I hear that I am in Italy! Wow! I am touring the Colosseum in Rome. I have seen a gladiator movie, so I know the Colosseum was where men fought battles against other men or animals, like lions. The guide tells us that this is the largest amphitheater ever built, and I believe it. The size is staggering. And to think that it was built thousands of years ago! I check and as I thought, Italy is located in south-central Europe. I was told by dad that one of our distant cousins traced a part of our family history back to 15th century Italy!

A cruise ship is where my next adventure takes place. I'm not sure how I feel as I look very far down into the murky waters below through a pair of gold-colored, octagonal framed eyeglasses. I can feel a gentle rocking. According to Nonna's journal entry of May 2006, I am standing on a stateroom balcony witnessing glaciers in College Fjord, Alaska. The ship is slowly turning, which allows a 360-degree view of this mesmerizing scene. Ribbons of clouds thread through snow capped mountains surrounding the inlet. The sun is warm and the air cool as I walk around this huge ship. There is food available 24/7, and I hang out at the dessert bar. Suddenly through the window, I see a large spray of seawater. I strain to see, and I am rewarded by sighting the tale of a whale as this immense creature dives into the sea. I know Alaska is one of our country's 50 states, but where is it? Looking at the atlas, I see that it is way above Canada. Now I know why it is so cold!

My last eyeglass adventure takes me to the green hills and valleys of Kentucky. I am sporting a pair of very tiny dark sunglasses. Nonna and Pop-Pop were there in May 2001, when they visited the world's longest cave at Mammoth Cave National Park. Stairs lead down to the cave which is of course... mammoth! Nonna wrote in her journal that the tour takes four hours, and there are lots of steep stairs, hills, and slopes. The caves have an interior temperature of 58 degrees all year round. I'm glad I have my sweatshirt. I hike from one cavernous area to another. Sometimes the trek is wide, sometimes narrow. Often the cave ceilings are so low you feel as if you are crawling. The tour ends in the Frozen Niagara Room. The name says it all, as you take in what looks like a towering frozen waterfall.

Stalactites reaching down and stalagmites stretching up. Nature is truly amazing!

Well, my cousins seem to take this news in stride. They both take turns regaling me of their own "trips" taken. Jordan then hands me a small pair of sunglasses. I put them on, but I am disappointed to see nothing more than my familiar surroundings. A different pair of specs, and again, nothing.

I'm not sure what to think when next I hold an odd-looking single handle pair of glasses to my eyes. Now this is awesome! I'm in a field under a cloudless sky. Squinting in the sunlight I can see a bison wandering through the high grass. Taking down the lorgnette, as Faith calls it, I can see both Faith and Jordan have seen exactly what I have just experienced.

The football game now forgotten, I grab all the glasses from my closet shelf. The girls try on every pair. To everyone's dismay, the girls cannot see any of my journeys. Why is that? Questions, ideas, and theories abound between the three of us. We suppose the reason we all can experience Yellowstone is that Nonna and Pop spent the most time there. Nonna spent hours writing about her time in Yellowstone and with considerable detail.

Oops... at this moment, the three of us look like little kids caught with their hands in the cookie jar. My dad just opened the door to find the three of us surrounded by antique eyeglasses!

LOGAN

I'm watching the Eagles play. It's Sunday in Philly and I'm listening to my dad and Uncle Paul banter back and forth. We are pounding down chips and salsa when dad asks, "What happened to Bray and the girls?" I have no idea, and since half-time is giving us a chance to stretch, dad and I go off in search of the missing.

I'm standing behind dad as he opens the door. We see guilty faces and eyeglasses. OMG! In that instant, I realize that the eyeglass journeys I assumed were my own are being shared.

Faith breaks the silence. She stands, hands the lorgnette to my dad, and asks him to look through the lenses. We hold our breath for what seems like a very long time. I can see right away that dad is being transported somewhere that isn't here. He takes the glasses away from his eyes. Not one for small talk, he simply says, "Someone better start talking."

I back away to my room returning with my stash of glasses. Faith and Bray are talking a mile a minute, and no one is making sense. Uncle Paul joins the raucous group and takes control. Each of us gets to talk in age order. Faith begins with tales of Yellowstone. You can now hear a pin drop, and I listen intently as this is my first time hearing about these fantastical experiences. No one is surprised when I finish up by telling my tales.

I show off a very small pair of gold, oval framed glasses with thin bendable arms. I relate how these specs transport me to Mount Rushmore in the Black Hills of South Dakota. The gigantic carved sculptures depicting the heads of presidents George Washington, Thomas Jefferson, Abraham Lincoln, and Theodore Roosevelt are something I have seen so many times in history books and on TV. Seeing this up close is amazing. So majestic! The carving is surprisingly detailed. I also go behind the heads (who knew?) to where the artist's studio is located. I see many of the architectural plans for the mountain and watch a movie on how the carvings were made. Coming down the path I see six very large bighorn sheep! They are moving effortlessly across the rocks and boulders. What a sight!

A pair of glasses that can best be described as ancient-looking green colored sunglasses take me to a place called Moab, Utah. I am speeding down the Colorado River in a jetboat. The boat eventually slows down so that the group onboard can see the towing cliffs on either side of the river. We see petrified wood and fossils at one stop. We float past Arches National Park and Dead Horse Point State Park, where rock formations are just astounding.

Another day another pair of "magic" glasses. These glasses are Pince-nez with cork lining the nose piece. Surprisingly they are very comfortable. They take me on a city bus tour of Washington D.C. The capital of the entire United States. I'm on the top deck of a double-decker bus. The driver/tour guide is taking us through the federal district. I see all the buildings I have studied in my classes. The most impressive one to me is the U.S. Capitol building. It is so much larger than I expected. The building is just so grand. We pass by the White House with its recognizable facade. Next, is the Lincoln Memorial. Again, I marvel at the immense size of the Lincoln statue! I'm blown away by the Martin Luther King, Jr. Memorial. His imposing figure overlooks carvings of his inspirational quotes in stone. D.C. is one of the most visited places in the world. I can tell you how I know this is true with one word: traffic!!!

My last journey is courtesy of rounded tortoise shell-framed glasses with wire arms rounded to fit around the ears. Ohiopyle is surprisingly not in Ohio. This Pennsylvania state park was visited by my grandparents in 1999. It was one of their first trips in their first motorhome. I found myself on another bike trip. This trip was so much more relaxed without those pesky Florida alligators! I'm riding on what Nonna refers to as a "rails to trails" path next to the Youghiogheny River. It's so funny to see people carrying their canoes because so much of the river is too shallow to boat. There was a drought that summer my grandmother noted in her journal. After a while, I take a break in a small market. I notice a group of people standing around a very old TV set. A special report is airing about the disappearance of John F. Kennedy Jr., his wife, and sister-in-law in a plane crash. Wow!

I quickly take off my glasses and Google the story. I see that Nonna took the time to record all the facts of this tragic story in her journal. Despite the event that day, my grandparents finished their bike ride, and so did I.

After I finish describing my "trips," Faith hands me the infamous lorgnette, and I too can see the bison! Uncle Paul is the last link and confirms that he too has been transported somehow to Yellowstone. Everyone is quiet, the Eagles game long forgotten. Dad and Uncle Paul bow out of the room to order pizza and attempt to calm down. You can tell they are truly shaken.

Bray turns to me and asks when did I first know about the glasses' power? We talk, comparing our stories. I also try on the glasses that the girls brought with them. In keeping with everyone else, I can't see any of their adventures and vice versa. The one thing we all have in common is the ability to stand in Yellowstone National Park. I feel good that we have all shared and know each other's unbelievable experiences. But...now what?

PHILIP

Never in my life have I been so shocked. Never in my life have I ever felt so desperate to understand. How can any of this be explained? Something was niggling at the edge of my mind. I put down my beverage and asked my brother to follow me to my bedroom. In a box tucked in the back of my closet, I found the item to which I was being mentally drawn. I lifted from a box a set of pictures and stones. After my parents returned from their Yellowstone trip that fall, Mom gave these packets to me and my brother and all four grandkids. I opened the note she wrote with each set and read: *"Nothing is to be taken from a national park. I, however, took these stones from the hot springs in the Gardner River. The picture included shows me holding the stones and the exact spot from where I pilfered them. I challenge all of you to one day travel to Yellowstone and put them back!"* She and dad spoke of their favorite national park with reverence, and they wanted all of us to experience nature's phenomenal beauty, Yellowstone style!

For several days, Paul Jr. (PJ) and I could talk of nothing else. We texted every day about the different theories that we had regarding the unexplainable phenomenon of the eyeglass journeys. Finally, we decided it was time to get Dad's take on all this.

PAUL JR. (PJ)

Our dad is a very pragmatic man. He doesn't suffer fools lightly as they say. This talk was going to be tough. Tough because all of this revolves around Mom. They had been married for 47 years and were very close. You can *only* be close in a 40-foot motorhome where they spent so many years together.

Philip and I walk into Dad's apartment and begin at the beginning of this mesmerizing and strange tale. The final piece of the story was asking dad to look through the lorgnette and tell us what he sees. The bison. He sees the bison and all the nature that we had also experienced.

He stands, places his hand on the urn that holds mom's ashes. "Looks like we are all going to Yellowstone." Dad's broad smile gives us all we need to know. Our mom is behind the wonderful strangeness. She is still with us.

POP-POP

The seven of us hop aboard our flight in Philly and land in Bozeman, Montana on a sunny afternoon. The next day we are off to Yellowstone National Park and Mammoth, the north entrance of the park. We hike out to the hot springs and quickly find the exact spot from where Susan had taken the stones. As each rock is thrown back into the spring, I silently speak to my wife's spirit. Although a solemn moment, it is a joyful moment as well. I feel Susan's spirit on the wind.

The hot spring lies within the cooler waters of the river. You have to situate yourself in the area where the two temps of water converge. If not, the hot springs water will make it very uncomfortable!

The rest of that week was spent with everyone either hiking, touring, fishing, or sightseeing. The park has over two million acres of land, but we hit the high spots. I was thrilled to take everyone to the Lamar Valley to see the bison grazing. This had been Susan's favorite spot. I could feel her with us every step of the way.

We never figured out the rhyme or reason behind which glasses saw which adventures or why only certain places could be experienced. We decided to simply accept that Susan left us all one amazing gift!

Our last night in the park we all sat around the campfire making S'mores and drinking hot chocolate. It had been a busy, fun-filled week. As we later looked up into the millions of stars, my granddaughter Faith quietly remarked, "You know, Nonna did love each one of us best."

THE END

OLD FAITHFUL GEYSER
YELLOWSTONE

AFTERWORD

think all of us want our loved ones to remember us after we leave this earth. If that were not true, sites such as Ancestry. com just would not exist. How do we accomplish this without our material possessions becoming a burden? Ask yourself this question, *Do I want all of my "stuff" to be offered to strangers at an estate sale?* It pains me to see lovingly collected objects sold for pennies on the dollar.

Let's talk about how you can make your most treasured items mean something to your loved ones. Do you have a collection? Don't get hung up on the monetary value. My aunt collected pennies of the year that significant events occurred in her life and folded each penny into paper listing the event!

Think of ways to make your collection attractive to display. All of my eyeglasses are attached to beautifully painted window frames enclosing "chicken wire." These frames are hung on the wall and make an interesting conversation piece. Go into any

craft store and you will see dozens of different ways to display items. Be it a shelf or a shadowbox, different designs abound. Go to thrift shops, antique stores, and yard sales. Use your imagination to display your treasured objects uniquely.

Do you have a collection of over fifty red-haired dolls? Whittle this down to three to five dolls and leave each set to a different relative or friend. Take stock of individual pieces you own. You may think the watch you wear every day isn't worth much. Your grandchild, however, may see the sentimental value in owning this reminder of you.

If you do have important pieces of jewelry, art, or furniture, make sure you designate in writing who receives these pieces. Preferably this is written in your will.

Provenance is established when we have proof of an item's origin. Include with each treasure a photograph of you wearing that piece of jewelry. Take a picture of that heirloom chest placed at the bottom of your bed. Personalize everything you wish to pass on by writing a short note as to the item's history. Attach the note and or picture to the bottom of the piece or enclose a smaller item in a box with the information. How did you come to own the object and how old is the piece?

Some items you own can be turned into useful items that a dear one will cherish. An old flannel shirt can become a pillow. A favorite scarf can be turned into a stuffed animal for great-grandbabies yet to be born! Make sure to include a picture of you wearing the item for maximum effect. Coverlets, quilts, throws, and blankets can be made from long-stored children's clothes and baby blankets. Very old suitcases, especially those with travel stickers can become end tables or display tables.

I could write a separate book on the many ways to leave useful and sentimental items to our heirs!

I hope this story and my suggestions will give you the encouragement and confidence to take inventory of your most cherished items. Our families are everything to us and you can share your history well into their future!

9 781936 885343